# Little Bridge Farm

## Tiger's Great Adventure

Tiger the tiny kitten just loves exploring
– but will she find herself in a fix?

Look out for all the Little Bridge Farm books!

# Little Bridge Farm

## Tiger's Great Adventure

PETER CLOVER

Illustrated by Angela Swan

SCHOLASTIC

First published in 2007 by Scholastic Children's Books
An imprint of Scholastic Ltd
Euston House, 24 Eversholt Street
London, NW1 1DB, UK
Registered office: Westfield Road, Southam, Warwickshire, CV47 0RA
SCHOLASTIC and associated logos are trademarks and/or registered
trademarks of Scholastic Inc.

10 digit ISBN 0 439 94464 3
13 digit ISBN 978 0439 94464 9

British Library Cataloguing-in-Publication Data
A CIP catalogue record for this book is available from the British Library

Printed in the UK by CPI Bookmarque, Croydon, CR0 4TD
Papers used by Scholastic Children's Books are made from wood grown in
sustainable forests.

3 5 7 9 10 8 6 4

www.scholastic.co.uk/zone

To Val and Mark

# Chapter One

A bright shaft of morning sunlight filtered down through the skylight in the roof of Big Red Barn. Tiger the kitten leapt up on to a bale of hay and sat in the warm puddle of light. Just beneath the bale, she could see her five brothers and sisters, fast asleep in a warm, fluffy bundle.

Their mother, a tabby cat, lay curled in the straw next to the kittens' wicker basket. Tiger wriggled with happiness from the tip of her nose to the tip of her tail. They all looked so peaceful lying there.

It was very early and all the animals in the Big Red Barn were fast asleep.

Tiger looked around. Oscar the pony was dozing dreamily in his stall. Filbert the goat was snoring loudly. And Smudge the Labrador puppy was cuddled up to Parsley the Jack Russell. Tiger was the only animal who was awake. She had the whole barn to herself.

"Grrr!" Tiger growled to herself. She liked to imagine herself as a big, fierce tiger stalking her brothers and sisters. She would never hurt them, though she often liked to creep up on them when they weren't looking. But they were all asleep. She crouched low on the bale of hay, wondering what it would feel like to pounce into the middle of the cat basket and wake them all up!

Tiger gave another low, grumbling growl, pretending that she was the bravest, scariest, most dangerous kitten in the entire world. It wouldn't be *so* naughty, would it, to wake her brothers and sisters up? They'd be awake soon, anyway.

Tiger bristled her striped orange and white fur into a spiky ball. Her kitten fur stood on end like the prickles of a fierce, orange hedgehog.

"Grrr!" Tiger narrowed her eyes and prepared to pounce.

"TIGER!" whispered a stern voice. "Don't you dare!"

Tiger peeped down over the edge of the bale of hay. There was her mother, Cider. She had one sharp eye open, watching her. Tiger should have known.

*How does Mum do that*? Tiger thought to herself. *She always knows when I'm about to be naughty.*

Tiger twitched her whiskers and made her short tail bush out like a fox-brush.

Cider gave Tiger a long, silent stare. She didn't need to say another word. Tiger knew if she carried on she'd be in big trouble.

Tiger decided not to pounce. Instead, she waved her tail slowly in the air. Then she jumped down from the bale and ran over to Cider to have her ears licked. Tiger didn't want to make Cider cross with her.

But as she cuddled up to her mum,

Tiger couldn't help one paw padding the ground in front of her and her tail still twitched. She was so full of energy. Just sitting still made her feel as though she would burst!

A large yellow butterfly fluttered in through the doors of Big Red Barn. Tiger watched it skitter through the air – up and down! up and down! – until it slowly flew towards Tiger. She didn't dare move and she didn't dare breathe as she watched to see what the butterfly would do next. Softly, it settled on Tiger's little pink nose.

Tiger had never seen such a beautiful butterfly before. She watched as the butterfly lazily opened and shut its golden yellow wings. The butterfly's feet tickled Tiger's nose.

*Oh no!* Tiger thought. She could feel what was starting to happen. Her nose itched and twitched. She didn't want the butterfly to go away.

"A... Ahh... Ahh ... choo!" Tiger sneezed. The butterfly shot off and fluttered away.

"Come back!" Tiger called after the butterfly. As Cider turned to lick behind the ears of one of Tiger's sisters, Tiger jumped up to follow her new friend. But it was too late. The butterfly flew through a small gap between the wooden doors. She was gone. Tiger huffed a sigh. Butterflies didn't make very good friends, she decided. She sat down and began to wash her nose with her paws. That always made her feel better.

Around her, the other animals began waking up, yawning and stretching. Out of the corner of her eye, Tiger could see Oscar in his stall. The pony's long tail swished below the gap in the stall-gate. That must mean Oscar was awake.

*That tail would be such fun to play with!* Tiger thought. As she watched the tail swish, she climbed to her feet. She took one step forwards, then another. . . She just had to do some more stalking! That tail looked such good fun to play with! Tiger flattened herself to the ground, lay her belly against the soft straw, and began to creep towards the pony's stall.

Tiger's ears pricked up as the barn's big wooden doors suddenly opened wider and Farmer Rob stepped inside. She froze and watched as the farmer walked over to Oscar.

"Morning, lad," the farmer said, giving Oscar a friendly pat on the rump. Tiger watched Oscar crane his head round to eat the sugar cube that Farmer Rob always brought for him.

Farmer Rob was taking the pony out for his morning run. Tiger knew she had to hurry if she wanted to get that tail. She kept her head low, her ears flat, and stalked her way quickly across the barn. The morning sunlight made Oscar's tail shimmer as Farmer Rob walked him towards the doors. Flick! Swish! Oscar's tail went back and forth. Tiger knew this was her last chance. She pounced.

"Yeeooowwwlllll."

She leapt through the air and stretched out her paws for a swipe at Oscar's tail. If she could just get one golden hair, that would be a brilliant prize for her stalking. But she was in such a rush, she didn't set off in a big enough jump. She could feel herself falling to the ground. Not yet! She was going to miss Oscar completely – and hurt herself. She fell to the floor with a thud. Oscar trotted past and out through the barn doors.

Tiger picked herself up out of the dust.

"Are y-y-you OK?" a sleepy voice asked. It was Filbert the goat, just waking up.

"Of course I am!" said Tiger, turning round. "I love playing in the sawdust." Tiger didn't want her friend to think she was bad at stalking.

"Oh. It's just that you looked like you might have hurt yourself," said Filbert, trotting over. Tiger ruffled her fur and tried not to look embarrassed. She could see that Filbert knew something was up. "Is there anything I can do. . .?" he started to ask. But Tiger gave him a look. Filbert didn't finish his question. "Do you have any food?" he asked, instead. Filbert was always hungry. This made Tiger feel better.

"Sorry, Filbert, I haven't," she said.

"Oh well," Filbert sighed. Then he went back to his stall.

Tiger shook the wood-shavings from her fur.

Then, Tiger noticed that the barn doors had been left wide open. And outside she could see the farmyard! She scurried over to the big barn doors, and peered out.

Her green eyes grew wide with excitement.

"Wow!" she gasped. "Just look at *that*!"

# Chapter Two

There was so much to see through the open barn doors. Across the farmyard, Tiger could see the pigsties and the wooden chicken house where her friends lived. Beyond them was the farmhouse with roses growing around its doorway. And beyond that were the green hills, stretching out of sight. Tiger didn't know what lay beyond. It was too much for her even to think about. There was so much here!

Tiger watched Oscar being led to his field. Monty the moorhen and Ernest the goose were laughing together in the farmyard. They'd probably been playing another one of their jokes. Tiger could see Parsley and Smudge yipping excitedly and chasing each other all over the farmyard. Everything seemed to be happening OUTSIDE Big Red Barn.

Tiger sat in the doorway, watching everything that was going on. There was so much to explore! It couldn't hurt, could it? She put one foot out on to the warm cobbles of the yard. Another foot appeared next to hers – much bigger. It was Cider. Tiger sat back down quickly, trying to pretend that she hadn't been about to do anything naughty at all. Cider nudged Tiger with her head.

"Tiger," said Cider gently. "You're not old enough to go outside the barn on your own. You know that."

Tiger looked up at her mum and nodded. But she couldn't help feeling disappointed as she followed Cider back to the cat basket. Her five brothers and sisters had all woken up now. Tiger watched as they wrestled and clambered over each other to suckle Cider's warm milk. Why couldn't Tiger be as happy as they were to stay put in the barn? As the other kittens nestled happily in the basket, Tiger looked over her shoulder. The bright sunshine outside seemed to be calling to her.

Tiger crept back to the open door.

"Remember what I said!" Cider called after her. Tiger looked back and nodded to her mum.

"I'll just watch, I promise," Tiger said.

Then Tiger heard a familiar clanking sound coming towards the barn. The milk pail! This was one of Tiger's favourite times of the day. She loved the thick, creamy milk that the farmer's daughter, Rosie, brought them. Tiger padded back and forth at the barn door as she waited impatiently.

*Clank! Clank!*

Tiger's striped tail twitched with excitement.

*Clank! Clank! Clank!* The noise was just outside the door. A shadow moved, and Tiger spotted a leg. Perhaps she could surprise Rosie!

Now!

Tiger sprang into the air, scattering straw everywhere. She wrapped her paws around one of Rosie's ankles in a big hug.

Rosie laughed at the little bundle of orange and white fur clinging to her right leg.

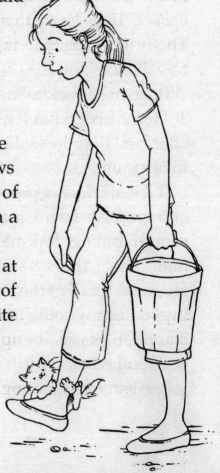

"Hello, Tiger. I knew you'd already be wide awake." Rosie waved her leg around and gave Tiger a ride through the air.

*What fun!* Tiger thought.

Then Rosie reached down and scratched Tiger behind the ears.

*Purr.* Tiger loved that! She rolled over on to her back, waving her paws and taking gentle swipes at Rosie's hand as the girl tickled her soft, pink tummy.

Then, Rosie dipped her finger into the milk pail and dabbed a drop of creamy milk on to Tiger's pink nose.

*Mmm.* Tiger licked her nose clean. The creamy milk was delicious.

Tiger followed Rosie across the barn and watched her fill Cider's saucer from the milk pail. Tiger watched as her mum dipped her mouth into the saucer and started to neatly lick up the milk.

"Woof, woof!"

Parsley came racing into the barn,

quickly followed by Smudge. They were playing a game of tag! Tiger leapt up on to a wooden barrel for a better look as round and round the barn the two dogs ran.

"You can't catch me," yapped Smudge, ducking behind a bale of hay then scooting between the legs of Daisy and Duke, the giant shire horses.

Tiger leapt off the barrel to join in the fun. She jumped behind a sack of oats, then quickly jumped out again as the two dogs raced past, bopping Smudge on the bottom with her paw.

"Gotcha!" said Tiger. "You're it."

Smudge barked playfully and chased Tiger round the back of some bales of hay. Tiger ran as fast as she could, struggling to keep ahead. She ducked beneath Oscar's stall-gate, mewing with delight as she tripped over her own feet and tumbled into the sweet smelling straw. Smudge pushed his head under the gate and touched Tiger with his wet nose.

"Now you're it!" Smudge declared.

Tiger raced after Parsley. Round and round they chased.

Tiger was having so much fun. But then the game sent Parsley and Smudge streaking out of Big Red Barn into the farmyard.

"Wait for me!" Tiger cried. But suddenly she had to skid to a halt. She was at the big barn doors.

Tiger knew she wasn't allowed outside. She sat down with a thump as the two dogs chased each other across the yard into the fields.

"But I was winning," Tiger called out after them. Her friends couldn't hear her. They were already running out of sight – and Tiger was stuck in the barn.

Tiger glanced over her shoulder. She couldn't see Cider anywhere. Then she looked back out through the open doors. Tiger had a thought forming in her head. An idea so daring that it made her heart thump wildly in her tiny chest.

"It couldn't really hurt," she said to herself. "Could it?"

# Chapter Three

Tiger stepped into the farmyard. She'd never been out here all on her own before. It looked much bigger now that she'd left the Big Red Barn. The cobbles stretched ahead of her and she could see that the fence was a long way off. The sky looked very big above her. She trotted forwards to follow Smudge and Parsley, but they were long gone. She couldn't see them anywhere. She was definitely too frightened to leave the farmyard and wander into the fields. Even Tiger wasn't that brave!

She turned back to the barn with a sigh. Then her sharp kitten eyes spotted something in the long grass by the fence. Something shiny, glinting in the bright sunlight.

*I wonder what that could be?* thought Tiger. She padded over.

It was Rosie's milk pail!

Tiger licked her lips.

*I wonder if there's any milk left inside.* Tiger slowly edged her way forwards. The thought of that rich, creamy milk was so good.

Suddenly, there was a loud BANG! followed by lots of popping and noisy rattling. Tiger ran to hide behind the milk pail as a rumbling tractor chugged past. Tiger felt the ground shake beneath her furry paws.

"That was scary!" Tiger said to herself. Six geese waddled past and Tiger stayed hidden behind the milk pail, waiting for her legs to stop trembling. She looked up at the milk pail. She could see a single drip of cream running down the side of the pail. She licked her lips thirstily. Now that she was here, she *had* to see if there was any milk left.

Hidden by the long grass, Tiger circled Rosie's milk bucket.

The pail was very big. Tiger was very small. She stretched up as far as she could reach, and was just able to rest the tips of her paws on the steel rim of the bucket.

But Tiger wasn't big enough to see inside. And the shiny pail was too slippery to climb. Her claws scraped and scrabbled but she couldn't get a grip.

She let go of the rim of the pail and glanced around. She looked at the wooden fence.

*That's the way!* she thought. *I can easily climb up on to those fence rails for a better look.*

Tiger leapt up on to the first rung.

She was a brilliant climber and soon scrambled up on to the second rung of the fence. Her needle-sharp claws scratched a hold in the rough wood of the post. The smell of pine filled Tiger's nostrils as she balanced on top of the wooden fence rail.

"What are you doing up there?" a voice called. Tiger nearly fell off the fence she was so surprised! She wobbled from side to side but soon found her balance again. She looked down and there was Smudge, running back and forth in the grass beneath her.

"I'm seeing if there's any milk," she said. "Sssh. Let me concentrate." Smudge gave a single yap and settled down in the grass to watch what Tiger would do next.

Tiger balanced on the fence and craned her neck out to peer down into the pail. Yes! A puddle of thick, creamy milk sat at the bottom of the bucket.

Tiger gave a mew of delight.

"What are you going to do now?" yapped Smudge.

"I'm going in," Tiger said – but she had no idea how! She was glad it was Smudge who had spotted her. He was only a young puppy himself and she knew he wouldn't tell on her.

Tiger dug her back claws into the wooden fence rail. Then she stretched her spine and reached forward to place her front paws firmly on the steel rim of the pail.

*Only cats can do this kind of thing*, thought Tiger, proudly. *Now, if only I can stretch just a little bit further.*

With one final effort, Tiger stretched as far as she could, and poked her head down into the pail. Her whiskers brushed against the milk at the bottom. She was nearly there! If Tiger poked out her pink tongue she would be able to taste the creamy milk.

Suddenly, she felt her back claws slip!

"Oh, no!" Tiger was losing her grip.

"Careful!" called out Smudge. Tiger wobbled on the rail. Her muscles strained as she tried hard not to fall over. Then she felt herself tipping forwards. It was too late. Tiger yowled as she tumbled with a clatter into the milk pail.

Splat! She landed in the middle of a milky puddle. Tiger sat up quickly and shook out her fur. She hated getting wet! Thick, creamy milk stuck to her fur, making it all cling together. This didn't feel good at all! She could hear Smudge barking as he ran round and round outside the bucket. Tiger was trapped!

# Chapter Four

*Oh no!* Tiger thought. *How will I get out of here?*

She looked up and mewed a loud, plaintive cry for help.

"Smudge? Help!" she called. Her voice echoed strangely. There was no answer. She couldn't hear Smudge's barks any more. Where had he gone?

Tiger scrabbled to her feet. She stretched up as far as she could reach, but still only managed to rest the tips of her claws on the rim of the pail. The slippery sides of the bucket wouldn't let her climb out.

Tiger looked up and yowled again. "Will someone please help me?"

"Who – who's that? W-w-where are you?" Tiger heard a familiar voice. But everything sounded funny from inside the milk pail, and she wasn't sure who it was.

"Smudge?"

Suddenly, with a clank of his horns, Filbert's hairy head looked down into the pail.

"Filbert!" Tiger said, relieved. "Please help me!"

"Oh dear! You've got yourself in a right p-p-pickle, haven't you?" stammered the scraggy mountain goat. "It's a good job Smudge came to get me." Tiger heard Smudge give a yap.

"I know," mewed Tiger, feeling very sorry for herself.

"And you know you're n-n-not supposed to leave Big Red Barn, don't you?" Filbert said. "Thank goodness you're a cat and you've got n-n-nine lives!"

"I want to go home," mewed Tiger.

Tiger had never been so glad to see Filbert's hairy whiskers or to smell his strong goaty scent. The goat laughed quietly to see Tiger stranded in the bottom of the pail. Then he leant forwards and gently got hold of the scruff of Tiger's neck with his long, yellow teeth. Tiger felt herself being lifted higher and higher up into the air.

Drops of milk fell on to the cobbles from Tiger's soggy fur as Filbert carried her back to the barn. Tiger could see between Filbert's legs that Smudge was following them as they made their way back.

They stepped into the barn. Tiger didn't want to think about what would happen next. She shut her eyes tightly as Filbert took her to Cider and put her down gently in the straw.

"I think this k-k-kitten belongs to you!" said Filbert. "She was out in the farmyard and she fell into the milk bucket!"

Tiger peered up at her mum. Cider looked very disappointed. All of Tiger's brothers and sisters whispered and giggled in their basket as Tiger sat there, dripping cream, looking sorry for herself.

Tiger waited for her mum to tell her off. But Cider shook her head slowly, and looked back up at Filbert.

"Thank you, Filbert," she said. "You're a real hero." Filbert skipped away, his hooves kicking up straw.

"I'm a hero!" Tiger could hear him saying to himself. Cider looked back at

Tiger. Then she began to lick Tiger clean of all the milk that was drying in clumps in her fur.

"It can be very dangerous outside Big Red Barn," said Cider softly. "You're far too small to be out there on your own. I know it's hard, Tiger, but you must stay inside the barn until you are bigger."

Tiger was trembling like a leaf as Cider lifted her gently by the scruff of her neck and placed her in the middle of her brothers and sisters.

The kitten's noses twitched at the smell of Tiger's creamy fur. Soon, they were all licking her clean.

Tiger giggled as their rough, pink tongues tickled her fur and made her squirm with delight.

Tiger purred loudly. It felt safe and warm snuggled up with all the others in the basket.

"I'll try much harder to be good," Tiger promised Cider, as she snuggled deeper into the basket. All the warm, soft fur around her felt so cosy. *It can't be that difficult to be good*, Tiger thought to herself. *Can it?*

# Chapter Five

The next morning, Tiger woke bright and early. The first thing she did was pounce on her five brothers and sisters.

"Let's have a wrestle," squealed Tiger, and the kittens tumbled in a mass of coloured fur.

"Tell us all about your adventure," said one of the sisters, as they all fell in a heap.

Tiger sat up proudly and puffed out her tiny chest. Things didn't seem so bad in the morning sunshine. Tiger could almost forget how badly she had scared herself. The other kittens huddled around her in the basket, waiting to hear.

"It was really exciting," began Tiger. She remembered the "Bang!" of the tractor. "At first, I had to fight a big, noisy, tractor monster!"

All the kittens gasped.

"You're so brave," they whispered.

"And then. . ." said Tiger. "I was attacked by at least one hundred wild geese!"

"Tiger!" Cider warned, as she groomed herself. Tiger remembered her promise to be good. She turned back to her brothers and sisters.

"But in the end, I realized how foolish I had been. We must never leave the barn without our mum to look after us." Tiger felt very wise.

"I could have told you that!" said one of Tiger's brothers. Tiger turned her back on him and pretended to start grooming herself too. Being good was hard work.

That afternoon, Tiger was playing hide and seek in the barn with her brothers and sisters.

"Coming to get you, ready or not!" she called.

Tiger knew all the places to search and all the best places to hide. She whizzed around the barn peering into barrels, under bales and behind sacks of grain. Then she spotted a small tail waving lazily from behind a wheelbarrow leant against the barn wall. She ran towards it and peered round the side.

"Found you all. That was so easy!" Tiger declared.

Her brothers and sisters grumbled as they piled out from their hiding place. "You're too good, Tiger!"

Then it was Tiger's turn to be hunted. Tiger considered the usual places: up in the rafters, inside Filbert's stall, the horse tack room. But then she saw the pile of wood that Farmer Rob had left just inside the barn doors yesterday. A new place to hide!

Tiger scampered over and discovered that there was a kitten-sized hiding place

just underneath the heavy plank on the top of the pile.

*No one will ever find me in there*, Tiger thought happily. *But how do I get in?*

There was a gap between the top plank and the next plank down, but it was small. Tiger tentatively poked her head through the hole. Her head fitted, but it brushed the ends of her whiskers back.

*Could all of me fit through there?* Tiger wondered.

Then Tiger remembered something that Cider had once told her. *If you can fit your head and whiskers through a gap, then your body will easily follow!*

Tiger sucked in her tummy and pushed herself through the tiny hole. It was a tight fit, but . . . by twisting this way . . . and stretching herself that way until she was really thin . . . Tiger managed to get her two front legs through. The wood scratched at her fur as she pushed the rest of her body through the gap, but soon Tiger was in the best hiding place ever, inside the pile of wood planks.

*It works! It works!* Tiger was delighted. *Mum was right!* Tiger stretched her paws out in front of her body and kept perfectly still. *They'll never find me in here!*

From her hiding place, she could see out of the barn doors. She watched the bustling in the farmyard as she waited for her brothers and sisters to find her. The chickens were scratching around the trunk of the huge maple tree that grew near the barn.

Tiger pressed her face right up to the gap. Beyond the barn doors, she saw the tree's leafy branches spreading wide and rising high into the air, almost to the clouds.

"Just imagine what the view would be like from up there," whispered Tiger to herself. She forgot all about hide and seek, and poked her head back out of the hole to get a better look at the tree.

Tiger heard some of the branches rustling. Something was moving in the tree. What could it be?

# Chapter Six

Tiger narrowed her eyes. She might only be a little kitten but she could see right up into the tree. As she watched, a wood pigeon stepped out from behind some leaves.

The wood pigeon looked down at Tiger and chuckled. "Are you trapped in there?" asked the wood pigeon from his perch. "A kitty with her head stuck out of the woodpile."

"I'm not trapped," Tiger protested, and squeezed and stretched her way back out of the hole. "See? I was hiding, but then I wanted to see how high the tree went."

Tiger had never spoken to a wood pigeon before, but she recognized him as one that Cider had chased out of the barn for pecking at Oscar's feed. Tiger stood on top of the woodpile inside the barn and watched the pigeon.

"It's great up here," the wood pigeon cooed to Tiger. "I can see everything. Even your mother prowling out in the field. Why aren't you with her, kitty-cat?"

"I'm not allowed out of the barn," Tiger explained, as the wood pigeon crept closer to her along one of the branches.

The wood pigeon stopped what he was doing and glanced over at Tiger in surprise. He looked Tiger up and down very slowly and cocked his head on one side as if he was thinking.

"What is it?" asked Tiger, suddenly

feeling a bit awkward. The wood pigeon looked away, as if he didn't want Tiger to see what was going through his mind.

"Oh, nothing," said the bird as he fluffed out the feathers on his chest. Tiger couldn't help it. She was really feeling curious now.

"Tell me!" she pleaded. The bird looked back round at her.

"Well. . ." He hesitated.

"Please!" Tiger begged. Whatever it was, she wanted to know.

"You say you're not allowed out of the barn. But perhaps you're too scared to leave the barn. Perhaps you're a coward," the wood pigeon said.

Tiger felt a growl rising in her throat.

"I bet you're afraid of climbing trees too, aren't you?" the pigeon taunted. "I bet you couldn't climb as high as me, even if you wanted to."

Tiger leapt to her feet. She'd show that bird.

"I can climb trees!" she said, feeling outraged. How could the wood pigeon say she was too scared?

"Show me," dared the bird. Tiger scurried out into the sunshine and over to the tree. No way was that bird getting the better of her!

The leaves of the maple tree rustled gently above her. Tiger sat at the bottom of the tall, leafy tree and glanced up at the lowest branches.

"Oh, that's very brave indeed!" called down the wood pigeon.

It sounded like the wood pigeon was laughing at Tiger. *Grrrr!*

Tiger put one paw tentatively on the trunk, and then with a deep breath, she streaked up the tree, her sharp claws scratching and scrabbling against the bark. Tiger soon found out that she was just as good at climbing trees as she was at everything else. She sat on the first branch of the tree feeling very pleased with herself.

"Purrrrrrrr! Purrrfect!" Her eyes opened wide. Her tail bushed into a bristling fox-brush. "This is so exciting!"

From the first branch, Tiger could look down on Old Spotty and Socks dozing together in their shady pen. She saw the hen-house with a big black rooster dusting his feathers on the tin roof.

"You're not even close to as high up as I am!" the wood pigeon said.

Tiger fixed the wood pigeon in her sights and climbed higher.

Tiger paused when she was halfway up the tree. Now she could see the vegetable garden beside the farmhouse, and the ducks swimming out on Pebble Pond.

"I don't think you're brave enough to come up to the top," the wood pigeon said, as he hopped up to a higher branch, near the very top of the maple tree.

Tiger climbed higher and higher. The treetop swayed as she clung on to the highest branches.

Finally, Tiger was on the same branch as the wood pigeon, who had waddled right to the end of the branch.

"See?" Tiger said proudly. "I *can* climb just as high as you."

Then she looked out across Little Bridge Farm. "Wow!"

She could see the trees of Albert Woods rustling gently in the breeze. Oscar galloped on Great Oak Hill. Willow

River snaked its way from the bridge to the distant moors. Tiger could even see the long muddy track that led up away from the farm. She wondered where it went.

"Fantastic! This is even better than I imagined." It felt so good to be high in the trees, seeing everything there was to see on the farm. Just perfect for a curious little kitten.

But, just then, the branch she was clinging to gave a terrible creak and Tiger's heart missed a beat.

"Cats are good at climbing up things, but not so good at climbing down. Now the kitty-cat is stuck in a tree!" said the wood pigeon in a nasty voice.

Tiger began to tremble. *Perhaps this wasn't such a good idea after all.*

Tiger looked over to the wood pigeon for some help, but the wood pigeon launched himself into the air and flew away.

"Goodbye!" he called.

Tiger couldn't believe it. What a rude

bird! She decided to get out of the tree and took a few careful steps backwards down the tree trunk. But Tiger soon realized the wood pigeon was right – trees *were* more difficult to climb down than up.

Tiger's foot slipped on the bark and she had to scrabble her paws quickly and grip the trunk tightly with her claws. *Phew! That was close!*

Suddenly, she heard a very loud bark and looked down. It was Trumpet. And he was looking up at Tiger, stuck in the tree!

"Tiger!" Trumpet called. "What are you doing up so high? Be careful!"

Tiger realized how high she was, and seeing how worried Trumpet looked made her feel really scared. She was suddenly so terrified that her legs refused to work any more. She was frozen to the spot – she couldn't move forwards or backwards.

"Don't panic," instructed Trumpet. "Come down nice and slowly. One branch at a time. Relax. And don't look down!"

"I'll try," mewed Tiger. She stretched out her back leg slowly, feeling for a hold on the thick trunk. She poked out her tongue as she concentrated on the downward climb. It was really difficult.

"That's it," barked Trumpet. "Take it nice and easy."

Tiger clambered backwards down one branch, then another. But then, her back leg poked into the hole in the tree trunk where Ollie the owl had her nest. She didn't mean to, but Tiger's paw landed right on the owl's head.

The sleepy owl poked her grumpy head out of her nesting hole in the tree and hooted angrily.

Poor Tiger was so surprised that she jumped with fright – and let go of the branch she was holding! Her body reeled backwards, away from the trunk, and her claws let go of the rough bark.

"Oh, no!" cried Trumpet in alarm.

Tiger paddled her paws in the air but she couldn't reach the trunk or any of the leafy branches.

She was falling!

# Chapter Seven

Tiger spread out her legs and bushed up her tail. But it didn't stop the ground from rushing up to meet her. Down, down, down she fell. She scrunched her eyes shut tight, not wanting to see the branches rushing by. The wind whistled past her ears.

*THUMP!*

Tiger was surprised to find that she hit something soft. She felt the tickle of woolly fur all around her. She snapped open her eyes. She'd landed across Trumpet's soft, shaggy back!

"Are you all right?" Trumpet asked, as Tiger climbed down from the sheepdog's back.

"I think so," Tiger said shakily. She had been very frightened by the fall. "I'm glad you were there to catch me."

Tiger realized that clever Trumpet had dashed under the tree just in time to break her fall. He was such a big dog that a falling kitten couldn't hurt him.

"Are you sure you're OK?" Trumpet asked, concerned.

Tiger flexed her legs, paw by paw . . . then she stretched her spine and her tail.

"Ouch!" Tiger said. On the end of her tail was a long scratch from the branches she'd hit on the way down. It stung when Tiger moved her tail. But she was fine. Nothing broken!

"You wait here," Trumpet said, "while I go and fetch Cider."

As soon as Trumpet was gone, Tiger thought of the look of disappointment on Cider's face when she found out what she'd been up to. Tiger knew she was going to be in such big trouble.

The wood pigeon suddenly swooped low through the sky and whisked past the front of Tiger's nose.

"Not feeling so brave any more?" he asked mockingly, before arcing up into the blue sky. Tiger watched the bird, and tried not to burst into tears. No, she wasn't feeling brave! The wood pigeon circled round and started to head for Tiger once more. She couldn't stand any more teasing, and she couldn't face her mum in the barn.

Tiger ran away across the farmyard as fast as she could, looking for somewhere to hide.

Tiger ran, and ran, and ran – around the side of the barn, through the milking sheds and behind a haystack. She wasn't even really looking where she was running. All the places that had at first seemed so exciting were frightening now.

Tiger stumbled and fell as she ran. She looked ahead and saw a long, wooden plank leading up into the back of a truck. The truck was loaded with hay bales and Tiger saw a cosy hiding place tucked away behind a loose tarpaulin. She ran up the plank and pushed her way through the tarpaulin into a dark, quiet space between the bales.

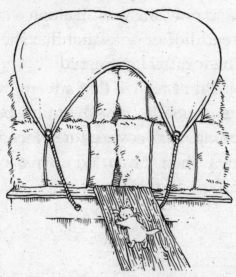

Her mum was right. Outside Big Red Barn, everything was dangerous, but Tiger felt safe now. It was warm and smelled of sweet, fresh straw. It reminded her of being back home in Big Red Barn, curled up in the cat basket with all her brothers and sisters.

Tiger trembled in the darkness. Her eyes filled with tears as she mewed sadly. Poor Tiger couldn't help it. She tried to be brave, but she suddenly started to cry. That fall had been really scary, and now she was all alone with no one to cuddle her or tell her that she was safe. She wanted her mum.

Tiger didn't realize that adventures in the big, outside world could be so frightening. She covered her face with her paws. Then she curled up in a lonely ball and tried to sleep.

# Chapter Eight

Tiger woke with a start, to the sound of a noisy engine bursting to life.

*Where am I?* It took her a moment to remember her fall, and then hiding near the hay bales. But now her dark hiding place was shaking and rumbling. She didn't feel very safe any more.

*How long was I sleeping?* Tiger wondered.

She heard a door slam, and scratched at the tarpaulin which covered her hidey-hole, pushing her head out through the opening. She saw the empty farmyard, and the sun dipping down in the sky. The animals were probably eating their evening meals. Tiger must have been asleep for a long time. Her mum would be really worried about her.

Just as Tiger decided she should go back to the Big Red Barn and admit what had happened, she felt herself moving. She looked up to see the farmyard getting further and further away by the second.

Tiger's eyes opened wide with horror. She had been hiding in the back of Farmer Rob's truck. The truck was loaded with hay bales. And now it was being driven out of the farmyard . . . *and fast!*

Tiger cried out for help. But the truck was beeping its horn and making too much noise for anyone to hear her tiny voice. Tiger stood, shakily, peering over the side of the truck.

*I could make a jump for it*, she thought. But it was a long way down, and the truck was moving much too fast to risk a jump.

Tiger looked back towards the cab. She could see Farmer Rob and Rosie sitting there, inside. She meowed loudly in their direction, but they couldn't hear a thing.

"What am I going to do?" sobbed Tiger, as the truck crossed White Stone Bridge and began to drive away from Little Bridge Farm. "How will I get home?"

Tiger thought of the view from the maple tree. The muddy track leading away from Little Bridge Farm was so long. Tiger imagined herself wandering along the road, no milk from Rosie, no cuddles from her mum. What if she got lost? Tiger longed for Big Red Barn and all her friends.

Suddenly, the truck went over a big bump. The hay bales shook and shuddered. Tiger flew up into the air and almost fell off the back. Just in time, she managed to catch hold of the tarpaulin as it flapped past her paws.

Tiger hung on tightly as the truck gathered speed and bumped along the road, tossing Tiger from side to side.

"Help!" cried Tiger as she clung on to the canvas cover. But there didn't seem to be anyone there to hear her pitiful cries.

*If only I had stayed inside the barn like everyone kept telling me!* she thought.

Then, out of the blue, Tiger heard frantic barking. She managed to glance sideways, and there, running alongside the truck, was Trumpet.

"Woof, woof! Hang on, Tiger!" barked the big dog as he raced faster and faster to get in front of the truck. Tiger screwed her eyes shut and hung on as tightly as she could, while the tarpaulin shook and bounced her from side to side. Her paws were aching. She didn't think she could hold on for much longer!

Trumpet barked and barked as loud as he could, pushing his way forwards to race alongside the cab. Trumpet gave a huge bark and Tiger could see Rosie looking out of the cab window to see what all the noise was about.

"Stop the truck!" yelled Rosie. "It's Trumpet! And he's trying to tell us something." Farmer Rob hit the brakes and the truck stopped so suddenly that the tarpaulin bumped against the loaded hay bales, throwing Tiger clear. She twisted and turned as she flew through the air, but luckily, with her cat-skills, she arched and twisted her back, stretched out her legs and landed on her feet.

Rosie jumped down from the cab to see why Trumpet was chasing the truck and barking so frantically.

"What is it, boy?" Trumpet was snuffling around in the long grass at the roadside. Tiger mewed sadly and Rosie soon found her.

"Oh, Tiger. You poor little thing. What are you doing out here all on your own?" She cradled Tiger in her arms and carried her back to the truck.

"It's Tiger," said Rosie to Farmer Rob. "I wonder what's she's doing so far away from the barn."

Trumpet jumped up into the cab and Rosie climbed in after him, cuddling Tiger to her chest. Farmer Rob ruffled Trumpet's ears. "Well done, boy." Then he turned the truck around and drove them all back to Little Bridge Farm.

Tiger's body hummed with purrs as she padded and settled down in Rosie's lap. She started to groom herself – first licking her paws, then washing her ears clean as Rosie soothed her with long, gentle strokes along her back. Tiger began to calm down, but she was still shaking inside. That truck ride had been a really nasty experience, and Tiger wanted to be back with her mum, snuggled in the warm, cosy cat basket. She couldn't wait to get home.

# Chapter Nine

Rosie carried Tiger into Big Red Barn and laid her gently in the middle of the cat basket with her brothers and sisters. Cider peered over the edge of the basket and gently licked the top of Tiger's head. Then she licked her ears and neck.

Two salty tears trickled on to Tiger's paws.

"Are you angry with me, Mum?" she asked.

Cider smiled gently.

"No, I'm not angry, Tiger. I'm just so pleased that you were found safe and sound!" The other kittens and all of Tiger's friends had gathered round.

Tiger had never meant to make everyone worry.

"Thank goodness that Trumpet managed to stop the truck!" exclaimed Oscar.

"Yes, Trumpet," meowed Cider. "I can't thank you enough."

Trumpet puffed out his woolly chest. "Oh, it was nothing," he said.

"We were all s-s-searching for Tiger," said Filbert. "But it was YOU who found her."

"I looked up at just the right time," he said. "And there was Tiger's head poking out from between the hay bales as the truck was speeding away. I had to do something quickly."

"We're ALL glad you did," snorted Old Spotty the pig.

"I'm so glad I'm home," mewed Tiger.

Cider gently licked away the remains of Tiger's tears.

"I've got a nice little surprise waiting for you," she whispered.

"A surprise!" Tiger perked up as Cider led her towards a ladder at the back of the barn. "Where are we going?" asked Tiger.

"Just wait and see," Cider said kindly as she urged Tiger to follow. They climbed the ladder up to the hay loft. "All your friends have been very busy up here!"

Tiger couldn't believe it! All the hay bales in the loft had been neatly arranged like stairs. Tiger purred loudly as she climbed the steps and followed Cider up the bales. *This is fantastic!* she thought. She looked behind her and saw all the other animals climbing up with her. Tiger could feel her tail bushing out with excitement. It was just like being on a hunting expedition with Cider leading the way.

"It's getting very h-h-high!" stammered Filbert.

"Just don't look down and keep moving," grunted Old Spotty.

When they finally reached the top, Tiger gasped.

"Wow!" She already knew about the skylight window in the barn roof. But the special steps led right up to a large wooden platform just below a window that Tiger hadn't seen before – only now the hay-bale stairs led straight to it!

"You'll be able to sit up here on the platform and look out across the entire farm," announced Trumpet. It was brilliant!

Cider had taken a blanket up there, just for Tiger.

"You'll be able to come up here and look out of the window as often as you like," said Cider.

"This is the best surprise, EVER!" meowed Tiger. She jumped up on to the blanket. Cider followed, and together they sat and peered down at the farmyard.

"Look!" said Tiger. "There's Rosie, going into the cowshed with the milk pail. And there . . . next to the farmhouse –

it's Parsley, burying a bone in the vegetable garden." A clutch of chickens flew up into the maple tree to roost in the dappled shade. There was so much to see from Tiger's special platform.

"You won't have to stay inside Big Red Barn for ever," Cider whispered. "We know you're curious and can't help it. And very soon, all your adventures will be real. But for now, it's very important that you stay at home until you're old enough to explore outside."

Tiger gazed out of her window. She could see Farmer Rob driving the truck full of hay down the road away from Little Bridge Farm. She turned to Cider, gratefully. "I'll never be naughty or run away again. No way!"

"I hope you've learned your lesson this time," said Cider.

Tiger snuggled up close. "I've had enough adventures to last me a lifetime," she promised.

Cider looked at Tiger and cocked her head to one side. "Are you sure, Tiger?"

Tiger looked out of the window at the pretty farm stretched out below. The day was drawing to an end and the sun was disappearing below the horizon.

"Well, enough adventures for *now*," said Tiger, cheekily. She nudged Cider playfully with her head, and together, the two of them watched the glorious red sun settle slowly over Little Bridge Farm.

# Look out for book four!

It was raining heavily. Water gurgled down drainpipes and into water butts outside Big Red Barn. Inside, the barn was warm and cosy and bustling with noisy young animals.

Old Spotty cleared her throat.

"Today, I'm going to tell my story from inside the barn. It's too wet to sit beneath the Telling Tree." The sow raised her voice above the excited chatter. "Quieten down now, please," she oinked. "Small animals at the front, bigger animals at the back. Let all the little ones through!"

Dilly watched as Tiger the kitten wrestled with her brother for the last seat on the cat blanket. A stream of yellow chicks bustled over to a pile of hay and made themselves comfortable, peeping quietly. Smudge the Labrador puppy settled down at the front of the crowd.

"Is that everyone?" Old Spotty asked, impatiently. "Dilly! You can't see from back there. Move up, quickly. I'm about to begin my story."

Oscar the young pony moved aside to let Dilly waddle past.

"*Quack!* Excuse me, please. Can I squeeze through?" Dilly pushed her way to the front, trying not to feel too

awkward as everyone watched her. She found a place to sit and shook out her wet feathers.

"Hey! Watch out, Dilly," squawked a gosling.

"Oops, sorry," said Dilly, lowering her head. She gave a final wriggle, waving the fluffy feathers in her tail. Part of Dilly's tail had been bitten off by a nasty fox when she was only a baby, and now there was a bare patch.

"Harrummpphhh! Ooof!" Old Spotty clambered up on to the square bales of hay set up as a platform in front of her audience. She pulled her trotters beneath her belly, and settled down in a wobbly heap. Then she flapped her leathery ears and everyone fell silent.

Dilly held her breath, waiting to hear the story.

"The Willow Farm Feather Race," began Old Spotty, "takes place every year." Dilly knew all about the Feather Race between the ducks, the swans and the geese. And in two days, they were going to hold the race again. Her brother, Racer, was taking part this time.

Dilly could feel a question building up inside her. Normally, she would never dare interrupt Old Spotty. Dilly was far too shy to call out. But this time… If she didn't get her question out, she'd burst!

"Is the race as dangerous as everybody says it is?" Dilly asked, thinking about her brother.

"Old Spotty doesn't like interruptions when she's about to tell a story," whispered Parsley, the tiny Jack Russell terrier.

"I know," Dilly quacked softly. Then she whispered quietly in Parsley's ear. "But my brother, Racer, is swimming this year. I want to know that he's going to be OK."

Old Spotty raised one white eyebrow and fixed Dilly with an icy stare.

"It's not as dangerous as all that. We wouldn't let youngsters race if it was. Now, if you've quite finished asking questions AND whispering among yourselves," grunted the pig. "I was about to tell you the story. You DO want to hear the story, don't you?"

"Oh yes! Yes! Yes!" exclaimed Parsley.

Old Spotty began again. "The Willow River Feather Race takes place every year, and the greatest race of all time was many, many years ago. That year, the contestants – Goldie the gosling, Silver the swan and Drake the duckling – had trained hard for the race for weeks. But the favourite to win that year was Silver the swan – she was by far the fastest cygnet on the river. There had been a lot of rain that week…"

Dilly listened hard. Dilly had never swum in the Feather Race herself, or ventured past White Stone Bridge – she was far too nervous. But she knew every centimetre of the course.

"The rain had made the river extra fast that year," said Old Spotty. "Rock Falls is the trickiest part of the race. And with all the extra water, it had become a raging torrent."

"Here comes the best bit," whispered Dilly to herself.

"The race was feather to feather all the way," said Old Spotty. "Drake Darefeather reached Rock Falls and swam the Gushing Gap to beat Silver the cygnet and Goldie the gosling by a beak's length! Drake the duckling won the race in style, claiming the trophy for the ducks."

"My granddad!" Dilly said. She looked over her shoulder at Drake, who stood at the back of the crowd. He gave Dilly a wink and she ruffled her feathers with delight. Dilly loved her granddad very much.

Dilly looked back at Old Spotty.

"And that was the last time that the ducks won the annual race. Every year since, the swans or the geese have taken the Golden Feather Trophy." Dilly could feel another question tickling her – just one last question that she had to ask.

"Who do you think will win this year?" Dilly called out, trying to make sure that her voice didn't tremble.

Old Spotty twirled her corkscrew tail. "This year," she announced, "all three swimmers look strong: Racer the duckling, Swift the cygnet and Glory the gosling. It could easily be anybody's race!"

The three contenders looked proud as they sat in the front row with their heads held high.

Dilly waved to Racer. The little black duckling winked at her.

Then Old Spotty called out, "Three cheers for the Willow River Feather Race."

All the animals cheered, from the little chicks in the front row to the giant shire horses at the back. The hens clucked, the dogs yapped, the kittens yowled and the piglets squealed.

"Hip, hip, hoorah! May the best bird win!"

PETER CLOVER

Little
Bridge
Farm

Smudge Finds the Trail

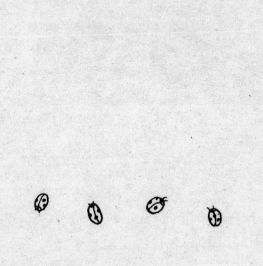

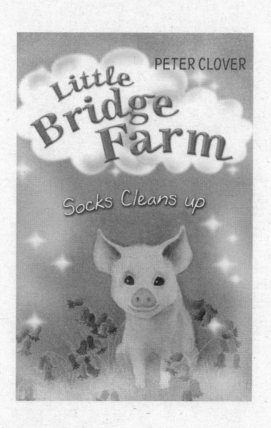

PETER CLOVER

Little
Bridge
Farm

Socks Cleans up